Mermaid Mayhem in Kerry

Patricia Forde
Illustrated by **Derry Dillon**

Published 2015
Poolbeg Press Ltd

123 Grange Hill, Baldoyle
Dublin 13, Ireland

Text © Poolbeg Press Ltd 2015

A catalogue record for this book is available from the British Library.

ISBN 978 1 78199 926 4

Cover design and illustrations by Derry Dillon
Printed by GPS Colour Graphics Ltd, Alexander Road, Belfast BT6 9HP

Mermaid Mayhem in Kerry

This book belongs to

- -

MAC – Mythical Activity Control

Mission Info

There was a time, long ago, when Ireland was a place of magic. Now, all the magical people and creatures live in the Otherworld. To people like you, they are just myths and legends. But sometimes they can escape into your world.

Mythical Activity Control guards the doorways to your world. And when someone gets through, it's MAC's job to bring them back.

From the Agent Files:

ÁINE *(pronounced 'AWN-yeh')*
Ancestor:
Áine, Goddess of
Summer and Light.
Personality:
Smart but stubborn.
Loves nature.
Can judge the moods of
people and animals.
Power:
Can talk to animals.
Can travel through
mirrors and polished metal.

FIONN *(pronounced 'Fy-UNN')*
Ancestor:
Legendary warrior Fionn McCool.
Personality:
Clever, sensible, but curious too
and that can get him into trouble.
Power:
Can connect to information from
either world by biting his thumb,
like his ancestor after he tasted
the Salmon of Knowledge.
Can travel through mirrors and polished metal.

TOGETHER, they help keep you safe from the
wild magic of the Otherworld.

Also in the MAC series

ALSO...

There are ten crabs hidden in this adventure. Can you find them?

The sea was calm. Muiris Feirtéir guided his small fishing boat out of Dingle Harbour under the light of a full moon. He headed towards Bull's Head where he was sure he would catch a good haul of mackerel. He was well out to sea when he heard it. Singing. But not like anything he had ever heard before. There was something otherworldly about it, something so beautiful that he couldn't concentrate on anything else.

He steered the boat towards the voice, closer and closer to the treacherous rocks. And then he saw her. A mermaid. Her hair was silver and fell in waves down to her waist while her deep-blue eyes shone like sapphires. She stretched her hand out, long white fingers beckoning to him. Closer and closer he went, bewitched by the music and her loveliness. He forgot about the fish, forgot about the boat, forgot about his family waiting for him back on dry land. All he

wanted was to go to her. He stretched out his hand. And then an almighty peal of thunder split the air. A flash of pure blue lightning followed it. The mermaid opened her mouth and laughed – a horrible sound. With that, the sea rose, tossing waves the height of skyscrapers into the fisherman's path. The waves were fuelled by a one-hundred-mile-an-hour wind that tossed the small boat about like a broken toy. Muiris screamed as he was thrown overboard and into the churning belly of the storm.

Luckily Muiris was later picked up, half-dead, by a fishing trawler and next morning gossip flew around the town of Dingle about the vicious mermaid who was luring people with her singing. Before Muiris, two of the Teahon brothers had gone missing, only to be found, zombie-like, searching for a beautiful woman called Mara. A week earlier an old man had destroyed his currach by taking it too close to the rocks over near the Blasket Islands. He was rescued and taken away, muttering about a mermaid.

Then suddenly, that morning, she appeared in the harbour close to the town. Everyone rushed to see her, with their cameras and phones. She didn't stay long but, such was the excitement, no-one noticed when two young people stepped through the hall mirror in Mrs Collins' famous guesthouse and hurried out the front door. They were Áine and Fionn, secret agents. They worked for MAC – Mythical Activity Control. It was their job to make sure no one from the Otherworld caused trouble in this world. News of the rogue mermaid had reached them and they were not happy.

At the corner of the street a television crew had set up their equipment.

"Well, this is something new!" the presenter was saying into the camera. "A mermaid media star! She was here posing for photos a little while ago! But she's moved on and there are astonishing scenes taking place in Kenmare as we speak. An entire summer school is walking into the ocean! Well, strangely, only the boy pupils are doing this."

"It's her! Let's go!" Fionn whispered, pointing at the large reflector the cameraman had used to bounce light onto the presenter's face.

Fionn and Áine only had to think of a place when they jumped through a mirror, or any kind of reflector, and the 'mirror roads' would lead them to the mirror that was nearest to it. Seconds later they burst through a mirror in a coffee shop in Kenmare. The café was empty but outside the beach was thronged with

people, all watching about fifty children, all boys, aged from five to twelve, wading into the tide. Teachers, parents, the Gardaí and the Coast Guard were all pleading with them to come back and struggling to hold them, but the children wouldn't stop. Their eyes had glazed over and their mouths gaped as they headed out to sea.

"Come on!" Fionn said and ran into the water.

But, when Áine caught up with him, she was shocked to see that his eyes were wide and staring, just like the children's.

"The singing," Fionn said in a dull voice. "I have to follow the singing ..."

Áine remembered the Greek legend about sailors putting wax in their ears to block out the singing of mermaids. She pulled a set of earplugs for swimming from her pocket and shoved them into Fionn's ears.

Then she slapped his face hard. "Wake up, Fionn!" she yelled.

Fionn blinked. "Where am I?" he said. "Hey, did you just slap me?" He rubbed his cheek. "And where did these earplugs come from?" He started to pull the earplugs out.

"No!" yelled Áine. "Don't!"

"Huh? Oh, good thinking, Áine!" said Fionn as he pushed them back in.

Áine could hear the singing now, coming from some rocks in the sea beyond the children. She beckoned to Fionn to follow her and dived underwater. Surfacing by the rocks, they saw a beautiful mermaid combing her hair and singing.

"Mara!" Fionn called.

But Mara dived into the sea as the sky darkened and lightning crackled then split the clouds with an enormous flash of blue.

As the sun came out again a large seagull landed on a rock right beside Áine.

"You want to talk to that wayward mermaid, I take it?" he said.

"Yes," said Áine. "We must get her back where she belongs!"

Fionn took his earplugs out and watched. It still amazed him that Áine could talk to creatures other than humans!

"Jolly good," said the gull. "She's a darned nuisance. Boats afraid to go fishing and all that. Makes things difficult for a gull."

"Do you know where she is?"

"Oh no, old thing! Haven't a clue. But a pigeon told me this morning that there's a goat in Killorglin who knows all about mermaids – he'd know where she is."

Áine frowned. "There have to be lots of goats in Killorglin. Which one?"

"Oh, that's easy! The one in the cage, old bean!"

"Killorglin!" Áine said to Fionn. "According to the gull there's an expert there. A goat in a cage!"

They swam for shore, found a mirror in a gift shop and minutes later they were tumbling into the bathroom of a hotel in Killorglin, completely dry as if they had never been swimming.

Out on the street, the place was teeming with people. And in a cage perched on top of a tower made from scaffolding was a big-horned goat.

Fionn stuck his thumb into this mouth, which was how he connected to information from the myth-web in the Otherworld and the World Wide Web in ours. "Killorglin," he said then. "Famous for the Puck Fair. Each year a wild mountain goat is crowned King and reigns over the town for three days."

"We'll have to climb up to the goat," Áine said.

"We can't!" said Fionn. "People would call the guards!"

Áine winked and smiled. Then she lifted her head and gave a low, sweet whistle. As she did a small bird dropped down and perched on her shoulder. Áine explained what she wanted. Five minutes later a huge cloud blew in over Killorglin. People looked up, mesmerized, as the cloud grew bigger and bigger. Only the agents knew that it was in fact a cloud of sparrows.

"Now!" said Fionn, and they climbed up the scaffolding tower as almost total darkness descended.

"Hi," Áine said to the astonished goat. "Can you help us? We're looking for news of a mermaid."

The goat's eyes narrowed. "Are you now? And for why are you askin' me about it?"

"We were told you know about mermaids."

"And what if I do?"

"We thought you could tell us –"

"And what's in it for the goat? Ha? What's in it for King Puck?"

"Well, what do you want?" said Áine.

"I want out of this cage, don't I? I want to eat grass and be free to roam where I want to, don't I? Look!" The goat shook himself hard and a beautiful pearl necklace fell out of his hair and landed by his feet. "See that? I'll give it to you if you let me out."

"We don't take bribes," Áine said sternly.

"All the same to me," said the goat. "I was told it has mermaid connections, but what would an auld goat like me know?"

"What's up?" Fionn asked.

"He won't talk about the mermaid until we free him," Áine told him.

"I guess we have no choice," said Fionn.

"Okay, King Puck," said Áine, "tell us and we'll open the cage."

"Skellig Michael."

"What's that?" said Áine.

"A rocky island off the coast of Ballinskelligs. That's where you'll find her – Mara the Mermaid. That was her old haunt long ago. Now let me out!"

Áine quickly told Fionn everything the goat had said as they opened the cage.

"I'll carry him down," Fionn said, struggling to get the huge goat up on his shoulders. "But be ready to run. I don't think the people of Killorglin will be too happy with us!"

Áine grabbed the pearls, fastened them around her neck and followed him.

Luckily, as the goat leapt off Fionn's shoulders and made off down the street he was pursued by a throng of people so the agents were able to slip away. Ducking into the local pub, they found a mirror and arrived in Ballinskelligs, more than a little out of breath.

Far out at sea they could see the steep rocky island of Skellig Michael, jutting out of the blue water.

Fionn put his thumb in his mouth. "Hey, there's an ancient monastery on the top of Skellig Michael," he said then. "It's a World Heritage Site. What's more, they shot part of the new *Star Wars* film there!"

"Wow!" said Áine. "Cool!"

Minutes later they were heading out to sea in a borrowed motor boat.

"Are you sure that goat wasn't spinning you a yarn?" Fionn asked.

Just then, a beautiful bottlenose dolphin sprang from the sea with a burst of loud clicks.

"It's Fungie!" Fionn said, jumping up and almost toppling the boat.

"Who?" Áine said.

"Fungie! He's famous! He hangs out in Dingle Harbour and entertains people."

"Never heard of him," said Áine.

The dolphin looked at her and his smile slipped. "I can't BELIEVE you haven't!" he said. "I'm Fungie! Everyone knows me."

"Sorry!" Áine said. "Haven't had the pleasure."

"This is more of it," the dolphin said, annoyed.

"Fame comes and it goes. Look at all the fuss they were making about that auld mermaid. Television crews, reporters! You could be jumping in and out of the water all day, and they wouldn't take a blind bit of notice, but give them a half-woman-half-fish, and they're gone pure MAD with the excitement. And even worse . . ."

"What?" Áine said.

"Sure two of the Dingle fishermen caught her last night. They have her all tied up out there on Skellig Michael and they've gone off to get a bigger boat – they were in a currach and they were afraid she might overturn it with her struggles. And the funny part is – they're going to make her into a TOURIST ATTRACTION if you can believe it. Ha! Like we need another one!"

Áine turned to Fionn and told him what Fungie had said. "These people don't know what they're messing with. We've got to get her back where she belongs."

"Well, you'd better hurry," said the dolphin. "The fishermen are on their way to collect her."

Fionn grabbed Áine's arm. "Listen!"

Áine held her breath. She could hear it – a high-pitched keening.

"Fionn! The earplugs!" she yelled.

"No, no," he said. "No need. She's not singing – sounds like she's crying!"

As they got nearer to the island, the keening grew louder. And then they saw her.

She was lying on a rocky shelf just above the water, tangled in a bright-blue fishing net, her beautiful eyes frantic with fear.

"Help me!" she gasped as the agents drew near.

Fionn and Áine jumped out of the boat and moored it. They could see that the net was held fast by a large anchor.

"Please," Mara cried. "Release me!"

Fionn frowned. "To do what? Haven't you caused enough trouble?"

"I know! I know I did . . . but I can't help it! It's my nature! Please, I only came back to find my . . ."

Mara stopped and stared at Áine, her mouth falling open.

"What?" Áine said.

"*My precious pearls!*" the mermaid screamed. "I lost them here in the old days. But there they are around your neck! Give them here!"

The agents looked at one another.

"Not until you give your word that you will go back to where you came from," said Fionn.

The mermaid frowned. She stared at the necklace.

The agents held their breath.

Finally Mara spoke. "Very well," she said.

Áine took out a small knife and cut the net. Then she placed the pearls around Mara's neck.

"Thank you for saving me!" Mara said and dived into the sea.

She surfaced, then raised her arms. Darkness fell instantly and a shoal of mermaids appeared, their scales sparkling in the starlight. They formed a guard on both sides of Mara. Then, with an enormous crash of thunder and a fork of blue lightning they were gone.

"Maybe the old goat did know something about mermaids after all!" Fionn said.

"All hail, King Puck!" said Áine, laughing, as she and Fionn made their way back to the boat and on to their next adventure.

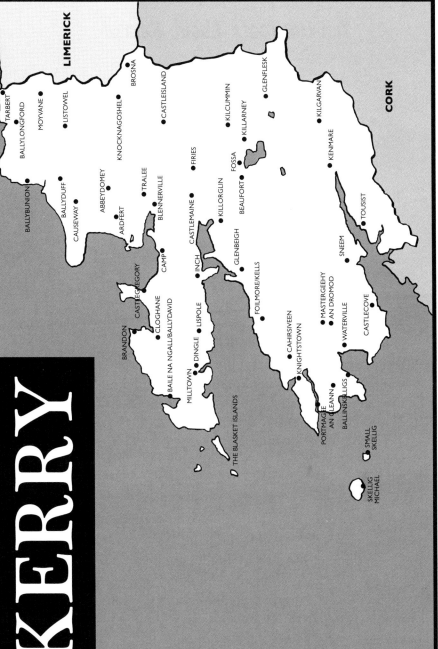

KERRY

LIMERICK

CORK

TARBERT
BALLYLONGFORD
MOYVANE
LISTOWEL
BROSNA
KNOCKNAGOSHEL
CASTLEISLAND
BALLYBUNION
BALLYDUFF
CAUSEWAY
ABBEYDOMEY
ARDFERT
TRALEE
BLENNERVILLE
FIRIES
KILCUMMIN
GLENFLESK
FOSSA
KILLARNEY
KILGARVAN
CASTLEMAINE
KILLORGLIN
BEAUFORT
KENMARE
BRANDON
CASTLEGREGORY
CAMP
INCH
GLENBEIGH
FOILMORE/KELLS
TOUSIST
CLOGHANE
BAILE NA NGALL/BALLYDAVID
LISPOLE
MILLTOWN
DINGLE
SNEEM
MASTERGEEHY
AN DROMOD
CASTLECOVE
CAHIRSIVEEN
KNIGHTSTOWN
WATERVILLE
THE BLASKET ISLANDS
PORTMAGEE
AN GLEANN
BALLINSKELLIGS
SMALL
SKELLIG
SKELLIG
MICHAEL

Ten Fun Facts About Kerry!

1. Carrantouhill is Ireland's highest mountain at 3,445 feet.

2. The Small Skellig island is home to 54,000 gannets, the second largest gannet colony in the world. 'Stormy', a storm petrel, is in the *Guinness Book of Records* for flying to South Africa and back to the Skelligs every year for 26 years – 10,000 km each way!

3. In 1730 a Danish ship, the *Golden Lion* was lured onto Ballyheige Beach by a false lantern light. The crew survived and the cargo of silver was put in a tower for safe keeping. But the tower was raided by 100 armed men with blackened faces. The silver was never seen again.

4. In 1965 Kerry's biggest baby was born in Killarney, weighing a whopping 15.5lbs. Charlie Nelligan grew up to be Kerry's greatest goalkeeper, winning seven All-Ireland medals.

5. Michael 'Butty' Sugrue from Killorglin was known as Ireland's strongest man. Among his feats was the pulling of a double-decker bus full of passengers!

6. In 2014, Kerryman Eamonn Hickson set the Guinness World Record for the 'Longest journey reversing a tractor and trailer', reversing from Dingle to Anascaul, a total of 17.5km.

7. Daniel O'Connell, one of Ireland's most famous men, was born in 1775 near Cahersiveen, and was known as 'The Liberator' because of his struggle for Irish rights. He was a politician and was against violence.

8. Famous 'silent film' star Charlie Chaplin and his family came to Waterville on holiday every year for over ten years. A statue of him is in the centre of the village.

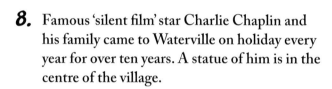

9. In 1977 the owner of Dromquinna Manor in Kenmare offered a reward of £50,000 to anyone who could rid his property of ghosts!

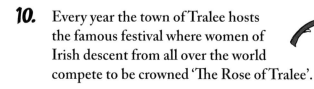

10. Every year the town of Tralee hosts the famous festival where women of Irish descent from all over the world compete to be crowned 'The Rose of Tralee'.

If you enjoyed this book from
Poolbeg why not visit our website:

www.poolbeg.com

and get another book delivered straight
to your home or to a friend's home.

All books despatched within 24 hours.

POOLBEG

Why not join our mailing list
at www.poolbeg.com and get some
fantastic offers, competitions,
author interviews and much more?

@PoolbegBooks